MW01675579

# Beyond The Fears of Tomorrow

By
Casey
Robert
Swanson

Beyond The Fears of Tomorrow

Copyright 2005
All Rights Reserved

First Printing
July 2005
ISBN#0-9773676-0-6

Written by
Casey Robert Swanson

Designed by
Gordon Swanson AKA Windward Design

Published by
The Dailey Swan Publishing

No part of this book may be copied or duplicated except with prior written permission of the publisher. Small excerpts may be taken for review purposes with proper credits given.

DAILEY Swan PUBLISHING

Dailey/Swan Publishing
1760 Liberty Street
El Cerrito, California 94530-3164

A special thought

to Luc

My Big Puppy

1993-2005

Where there is one

ending

Let there be a

beginning

Dedicated to

Jessica my wife. without whose

love and support

I never could have

finished this.

CRS

# Beyond The Fears of Tomorrow

# Chapter 1 ~ Prologue

The Netherlands
That which cannot be
Lands of the Lost Mystics
Home of the Indomitable Host

A quest into the beyond
To Find a journey never told
to the farthest reaches
To see what may be found.

To learn if that which exists
or has never been conceived
But in our minds totality
Can find its presence sustained.

From yesterday to beyond tomorrow
Always belonging to the past or future
With a present that can never be
In an evolving universe beyond our own.

Eller by your name and graces
Be not lost in the infinite wastes,
Perishing in the absence of thought
You must climb to find the light.

Eller stands by a door that cannot be
Motionless in a time that knows no ending
Pondering a question, Fathomless,
"To where shall I go for my Survival?"

He stands and waits with infinite Patience
As an eternity passes around him
Like the Wind blowing past a tree
For the question he has needs answering.

As he stands upon the edge of a precipice
The answer to his question, when it arrives,
Is far greater than a single mans being
It pulls him through, to the darkness beyond.

In answer Eller was given an insight
That a man, when given a new path for thought
Will create something original from past events,
And bring fourth to the future new horizons.

But when this new chain of thought is broken
With but the little that is of mans origins
Then that man will soon be dependent
On the thoughts and events which surround him.

And of that which could exist tomorrow
In the orderly creation of the future
Naught would be directed to the center
To the thought streams of the individual.

For Eller, his old world disappears
As he wills to be pulled through the dark gate
Into a universe beyond the image of man
Where nothing had existed but the moment before.

The emptiness of the space give him a unique feeling
Eller is now cut off from all others
His mind is set adrift, to wonder without course
Into this sea of Nothingless, his mind penetrates.

Can the human mind understand such a thing
With its limited scope and definition
The absolute knowledge that it is suddenly alone
In a universe, alien to past experience.

Within these thoughts Attained
Imposed by past wisdoms gained,
By those who fail to believe
In a minds potential to expand.

Are minds that are often held captive
Without the benefits of thought
Which can neither understand beyond
Nor experience in their surroundings.

Ellers mind roams, now freed of all restraints
Released from the bounds that had held so tight
For now was the feeling that all could be real
True in their own beliefs, proven in the own reality.

Ellers mind drifts aimlessly
In a search without beginning or end
To direct his way upon some chosen path
Of this no mortal can hope to achieve.

Drifting he is, without time nor dimension
In the limitless space of another universe
How can we try to follow his path
When we can never know which way he turns.

It seems that we are caught
In a web of indecision
That leaves us lacking in the spirit
To produce new action and follow.

At first I knew where Eller was heading
But now this needed foresight is gone
To provide the guidance that we now need
Can only be the job of Eller.

So let us begin now this voyage
by questioning the essence that is I
And letting this story be told
By he who knows it best.

And so Eller begins his Saga,
"The clear morning air is but a memory
Standing no longer on the ground am I
Above flies the spirit that laid within me.

I had felt an emptiness
A weariness that surrounded me
I had begun a search for something I felt
If only for a moment, but I could not reach.

In the world where I stood in my time
I was held back by all around me
Unable to rise above it's mediocrity
I was forced to let go of my freedom.

I had been caught without restraints
By the ties of tradition and ceremony
Unable to think beyond them to the future
Lost in the pretense of the past.

My senses of the world around me were lost
I did not possess the same assuredness
That those around me had learned to adhere to
Where that all we see around us is real.

I had begun to sense something beyond this
Something I knew could not be, unnatural
But there it stood, before my being
My senses reeled without comprehending.

I foresaw a destiny I had not known before
But I knew not to where it led
How was I to find without knowing it's direction?
In a world alone I stood silently waiting.

There are no strengths nor weaknesses
When there is no time for either
This then I knew, as I stood in patient sorrow,
To be the truth with it's lonely disposition.

Levels of knowledge, each greater than the next
To be attained by all who know their meaning
I passed beyond one with empty disregard
And stood now at the door to the next.

I questioned the reasons for my existence
For the present there stands too few answers
And if trapped in the present with the knowledge of yesterday
We cannot move beyond today to our future.

Cause and it's effects on all relationships
What is it to be alive and never knowing
I began to understand in a limited sense
Why a man cannot think beyond today.

Expanding that present past yesterday
I found these limits could no longer be
And what I saw maybe found tomorrow
By stepping beyond our world to another.

External surroundings mixed with tempered barbs
Invaded my mind and its reason to think
Challenging my existence in its everyday plane
I entered that which I could neither know or understand.

The non existence of this space
What could be the truth in honesty
When that which I knew before in my being
Could no longer be, as I stood before entering.

Assuming that all has been or can be
My soul opened into all of it's depths
And my mind crossed a widening chasm
Over a bridge of thought to tomorrow.

Into this strangeness I feared not to tread
In an unknown Dimension with only discovery to find
There will be something always to hold my mind
On the unexpected course that I follow.

Reality is for me now but a contradiction
I have stepped wholly beyond it's bounds
Into revelations that I could never know
Beyond what is real for a man, or could ever be.

Knowledge intensifies with each step that I take
While that which I hold within me yearns to escape
My mind remains no longer enough for my purposes
As I am the Alien where I now dwell.

What can be the origin of this Universe
If nothing exists within it's bounds
Before I entered on michapean chance
I must be it's creator, it's GOD.

I question the lasting ability of the space
Which I have entered beyond the old
Time no longer holds onto it's meaning
This space will last forever.

Why is it that no-one can ever be certain
Where our true state of existence lies
And why it will take us on uncharted paths
Until it is too late to understand.

Coming from a past and a present I know
Into a future that is mine to create
I gaze into the depths of my opening soul
To find my own meaning within.

For if I am the creator, the God
To build this Universe as I desire
Can it be this, that I may begin
Before the perfection within myself may be found.

Future expectations, lasting dreams
These we hold deep within us all
And so I begin my search with infinite care
My Future to be Found within this space.

# Chapter 2 ~ A Beginning

My mind longs for stability
Once torn with raptons confusion
It now lays sheltered with lonesome tranquility
Left without passage of time or thought.

Trying to sort out my minds differences
Sifting for all signs of doubt
I feel within me heartfelt remembrances
for what might have come before.

Enchanted paths cross stars with out meaning
Holding a course for my mind; carried
Left to myself in creating anew
I remember the old ways that led to destruction.

I gaze out on this universe that beckons me
Where there lies nothing to hold me back
Not even a beacon protrudes, pointing
To show where it is I lay, waiting.

What was to come in my creative cycle
A moment was needed to steer my way
And for those who were to follow after me
A guide to lead, rapture comprehended.

Testing those merits false and real
Of those dreams and goals I perceive
In this my Universe, still unscored
For my creation to follow, all needs to be true.

I search inside my mind and being
For any sign unnoticec to be revealed
Determined am I that which I intend to create
Contain none that will tarnish my dreams.

A better life around me I seek
Past Failures, none to hold court
Beginning anew in time is my guest
Achievement great awaits me.

Why is it to , that in trying to think
As we are all so often inclined to do
We can become lost when we try to comprehend
Something that we perceive so far above us.

A New Universe stands naked before me!
Awaiting my thoughts for it's creation
While the imminence of the project before me
Gives me pause to stop and reconsider.

The peculiarities of the universe surround me
with the personality of my mind joining in
How can I create something new here
When I am so much apart of the old.

A place to hold my existence
A home for my thoughts to coalesce
What's needed in this pretext of new
Is to create a new world from without.

And so do I quake within my soul
Torn by the ambiguities of this task to follow
Lost in the emptiness of this universe
Overwhelmed by the lessons of my mind within me.

I tear at the fringe of my consciousness
Endeavoring to regain my sight
Of that which I saw briefly before me
On the creation of the world that I seek.

Old moments glory first sustained
One main adventure laying within me
Whose purpose and meaning must be recovered
To retain what has long since been lost.

Guiding myself from where I now stand
To cross without fear uncharted shores
Still never really knowing where I am
And in which direction I am moving.

To where it is now that I once referred
Was it the past, the present. The future
Where my adventure began so long ago
And I was first thrown into my present state.

Twilight shades and expressionless symphonies
Bold new colors on a jaded beach
From one to another my mind now flees
Unable to chart other than a perilous course.

What is this that has happened to me
Since I entered this realm beyond old?
Where are my dreams and perceptions?
Are they gone with may old reality?

I was thrown out thru my improprieties
And now create a universe of my own
Proceeding at once from the beginning
So that I can know from where I once stood.

The rebirth of a Sun that I once knew
Now to be called Home Star, There shall I live
Brought out from my memories far behind
To lay guidance to the distortions of my soul.

With this object now before me
Glowing radiant with its golden light
My mind now at rest knows its place
In this universe of my creation.

To tasks now at hand need completing
Construction to begin on so much
All can proceed now on the course I set
With Home Star standing guard on my path.

My minds work begins to coalesce
Upon the beauty of the world of my dreams
And into this new-built horizon stretches
An ever present belt of vibrant green.

Green strands are grass where I lay
My sky above remains a bluish grey
Still tied to the past so it seems
My new reality is but a remake of the old.

Clouds form in unison above my eyes
Distant in the sky they seem to me
Reddish brown now in taking shape
I have caught them in a new realities light.

A struggle to follow now seems certain
From my wishes to create a world somehow better
Though tied to past memories I may seem
I strive in my creations to be free.

Before the infinite endeavors may begin
Creating a universe where none stood before
I must solve such problems in my mind
Defining and shaping what will come.

A Star holding my spirit is above me
Next inside to find my wants and needs
Then I can make a true planet fall
And begin my home system, for me to dwell.

# Chapter 3 ~ Home Birth

As I float in forsaken serenity,
Above this landscape that is mine to create
I question no longer the time as right to begin
As if time had any meeting left to challenge.

An immense flood of loneliness overcame me
From where I was I came to well know
That a man cannot live in emptiness forever
I must change this universe somehow I knew.

Mine to possess this universe
For me it had long since been created
From the open caverns of my minds soul
And in the need to create past fears.

Injustices that had been thrust upon me
As part of my past became my reality
These were what I had to grow beyond
In casting out my mold to work from.

Now was the time for a beginning
To create something from the hopes of the old
A world, a universe around me I sought
With those who would share all it's virtues.

Suffering and sacrifice of the old world
No longer could I hold this within me
As man conquered man and nation, nation.
In ever more frightful and destructive ways.

Domination and greed led to all sins
Horror and pain I saw all around me
The certainty of more throughout my days
Had driven me away from a future of pain.

Powerless and without hope in my old world
Feeling the sorrow of each hurt even more
I escaped for survival to my new world
And now will create no more of the old.

That which I had found wanting before
Could now be made to stand firmly beside me
Irrevocable as laws of nature that stand
Carved to be the laws of the new set out.

I think back now to my origins
On the myths of creation in my old world
And wonder to myself if I am only following
But the steps of those who had come before me.

Could it be that each world, each universe
Was but the creation of some other lost soul?
Some entity who had lost faith in his old world
And found a way to start over as had I?

A planet to begin in my image of greatness
A world to be called Home for my longings
A perfect place created from within me
To call my own for all time to come.

A workplace for tasks yet unknown
That will follow as thought become realized
I follow the signs that guide me
On a course the gods laid out before me.

Distant thoughts intrude their way
Distant themes remain intact before me
For the journeys end to truly begin
The truth revisited must be Homes birth.

Of this land that is due to be
Where I am God, it's creator
To all that will follow within it
I will be the soul and father.

Songs of eternity that have no ending
Words of love that contain no meaning
The jungle clamors for it's reincarnation
For the suns rebirth means it is next.

My quest is in search of honesty
Right to call my own in life
Wrong to be chanced as tilted windmills
On star-lighted pathways horizons lay.

Pave the passage in the ways to follow
The search that is mine and set to begin
From the currents of my mind embodiments flow
To create anew in the void, that is my home.

Journeys such when costly undertaken
Belong no wonder to wise mens dreams
It is the minds of the savage to discard
In my creations my thoughts tend to wander.

Children of paradise, knowing their dreams
Long since lost to melancholy horror
Staying off the path of righteous honor
I give you rebirth, go where truth shall linger.

My children, paths of destiny lay before you
Your dreams with my guidance now shall be
Mistakes of the past gone, rewritten works
Wrongs retooled to the future we seek.

Children it's said in sympathy
That follow a path to their destiny
Their fates are so cast as no inquiry
Who is to choose the path they must follow.

Guidance may come to those who seek
From many a source, my own incomplete
Their final destiny in the march of time
Lies in no hands but their own fragility.

A family of many shall be arisen
In a society of one where sharing is stronger
That which must be brought forward to the future
Is that which must never be forgotten.

With work begun I stand upon a high place
Looking down from these new heights with pleasure
I see the world that lays yet dormant beneath me
Amazed by the immencement of the sight.

Compared with that which I longed for
And all that I had ever known in the old
There lay in this new world a Majesty;
I was lost in the grandeur of my efforts.

I who had been once but a man
My feet firmly placed on planet Earth
Unable to see over the horizon
At that which lay beyond my sights.

Now I stand with my head in the stars
On the world of my own creation
Looking down on a new home for my wisdom
My own private dominion to lord.

Of the tasks that lay now before me
From the dreams of what is to be
I've been released from an ancient damnation
Of not seeing beyond my own soul.

# Chapter 4 ~ A Chosen People

Watching makes no difference to my minds reality
Right may be wrong if neglected
And a wrong may be righted with proper courtesy
As the way to the future comes unraveled.

A great birth now takes place
As people born anew will test my dreams
From the best of my past memories
Are the Founders to be chosen.

Pitched from the many of my past history
That I once knew so long ago
These are the few to be put into the future
Once released by me I can only follow.

From broken paths it may seem
That changes of thought often be
Before the wisdom of today beckons
It leaves my words untouched when called.

So I try to find in my future hope
A journey set with new beginnings
From the best of an earlier day they come
The people to lead the path that is chosen.

They are brought into greatness
Reborn to start anew
From my thoughts of likenesses
My world populated was to be.

The changes that I see before me
Amaze even the God within my casting
As my creations move from one to another
And take their charges from me.

From the character that they display
To the charity of their interactions
I knew my choice to be good
With each their movement of body and soul.

A vision of citizens likeness to be
Dark green grass laying over the land
Clouds overhead look quietly on
From the deep blue skies that are my eyes.

Moon and stars gather briefly
In the reconstructed world of my thoughts
They bring back to me memories lost
Of where I had stood once before.

In the eye of a hurricane planets rest
Lost passions lay inviting to caress
Waiting to explode in a vividness
Into the greatness that could possibly be.

Be in this guise of tranquility
The ashes of the good from the old are torn
Waiting to be reborn again as openness
Throughout the sounding of all time.

Urgently moving form one place to another
Greeting some worlds while letting others fall
To lay in some peaceful slumber at night
Of this I now hold a longing for.

But much must be done in preparation
Before I may rest once again
As a creation that is set into motion
Must be carried to its logical end.

Irreverent thoughts must be forsaken
Of a god I knew in moment alive
To grow into a belief beyond yesterday
May be a measure of man's greater good.

Titans of time that stand before me
Giants in our dreams slumber night
Semi-conscious thoughts pervade our waking
A reality within our context of dreams.

Around the life of the village sat
Crazed with excited expectation
A traveler of the deserts found
Here an oasis of intelligent being.

Not still-bourne a society crosses the lakes
Springing west like a jewel faceted star
Mired in the realization of a tomorrow
Once hoped that could never be.

Timeless quests and legends grow
Fighting to preserve their independence
Islands of thought discovered anew
And always with my fate before them.

Unmaking of the past seldom changes
Forgotten points of historical charge
A history of Birth not forsaken
And a greatness achieved without end.

Floundering Sometimes, somewhere
A world may shake inward to its being
But my thoughts moved onwards always
From the haze of my regrets to the future.

Journey on now without remorse
Though the lightening often strikes quickly
Into a realm of hope that this Universe
Could be created without the crisis of the old.

I have fought against this madness within me
Knowing that it could overtake me in my dreams
And have created a new holiness without fault
And a Home once again could I have.

A crossing venture betrays me never
A perilous start lays behind
Now next to me a golden opportunity
Within an imperial warning lies my world.

The rise of a city to greatness
No corruption of state can their's be
Revolt of the Republic never happens
Ageless it never ends so it seems.

Memories of a dream of mans great quest
To go beyond this I find I cannot do
The meaning of life unexpected
Create something new where stood none before.

Anxiously watching from my high vantage
As fortunes unfold before me
Should I interfere with the lives of these good people?
Or let fortune take its unknowing toll.

Rhymes of the wind in the wilderness
Waves of sand on the beach
The music still plays through creation
Endless harmony of goodwill to come.

What begins tomorrow for my people
Of this they can never know
But to join me soon in the forever
So their fate shall be predetermined.

Wisdom of a fashion I lay before them
Through the meaningless songs to the moon
This is all that I may give them to follow
For a journey known never starts anew.

Understanding the past in my venture
To the future will bring only hope
Not once doorways forbidden shall open
that our dreams go and whence are lost.

Cross winds and unexpected paths
A lightness in my mind now lingers
A crowd gathers before me
In this my foremost square.

Lost in the horizon are mysteries
Blacked out by a monument to reality
Two moons hang in the sunset
Five stars hang in the balance.

Impatiently waiting for my word
The priests gather now in the ways
To single out my last promise
How dare I to answer their calls.

A compulsion for wit
A greed for the beautiful
All has been lost in my quest
In a sprint for the greatness ahead.

To have all men as their brothers
Of this I have in creation tried to make
A world without evil has no bounds
Where goodness can always take root.

From castles tall to their villages
My mind had cast into being
A wold so fair that comparisons envy
Of that from which I had stood once within.

Noble king and mighty peasant be
The people of home grew as one
I smiled as I looked down upon them
'from here shall my universe begin'.

A grace I gave to each
A honesty true to be fair
A desire to build right, a foundation
Instilled within each a belief from conception.

To spread their seed lay their destiny
Their own world, then all others
Till the ends of the universe be reached
And the emptiness gone from my soul.

Such was my plan in its glory
That I cast, tendered before them
Put forth in my actions through this universe
Where dominions many were to be settled.

Seven days came with dreams outlined
Seven nights fell over journeys begun
So go the legends of old mens thoughts
In a past so dim as lost recounting.

Kingdoms will rise and fall in order
To rise again to much higher standing
Each time growing stronger with virtue raised
Such people as gathered in Humanities Age.

The choices to be taken are many
The paths to be crossed are few
My people in Freedom of Forethought
Begin soon to make these their own.

And I in my rapture stand watching
Of such beauty unable to believe
How can I a man such as myself
Have created a thing such as these.

# Chapter 5 ~ A Destiny Created

From the beginning beyond yesterday
To an infinity never to be crossed
Many paths now lead before them
Decisions great am I forced to make.

Beyond the wasted lands of my mistakes
Across the silken sea of pride
A lasting hope arises within me
Also now they make me a deity.

Graven wisdom upon their minds
Filled with false hopes and dreams
Many still are lying in wait
For unknown warriors to try and take.

False Gods many to whom they pray
I am not the God for them
Though this may be the Universe of my soul
These creations of mine know no bounds.

Puzzles of treasures awarded
I leave these for each tribe to find
And in finding grow to maturity
In ways that I cannot foretell.

Capricious lies lay cast around
Leaving lasting impressions still
With loves that may be forever lost
In idles time deigned wasted.

Adolescent dreams of childhoods lost
A strange hierarchy of misshapen thoughts
With lasting worn impressions still
Of tales torn and riches gold.

Colonial adventures in systems far
In these that are just beginning
Now I must try to cast adrift in trial
My worlds to live or die.

What shall they become in seeking
It is their destiny I try to guide
Sewn from seed as they came from within me
New heavens will be given or hells remade.

Even now as I watch them scatter
Across a wide universe to lay conquest
The was here, but yesterday it seems
A lone world standing at the center.

I watch them learn their new crafts
From the clues I have left amongst them
Will they ever reach, so long to go?
The final page of my ancient summons.

A return to their future assured
As in one of these many days gone by
Experiments that I have lost to impatience
Can never hope to be regained again.

A tradition of turmoil I requested
My mind knew of no way to focus
Just what it was needed, in vain?
But always what lay underneath arriving.

Life it was that I once loved
Now crying out in pain once more
A return is certain to unwanted ways
And what it was that had come before.

Now as Eller I must move on
And in trying conquer a universe
Created solely in my dreams
It created also from my fears.

A paradise here had seemed certain
This that I had tried so to make
But having lost in now it seems
On a shorter path not wisely taken.

A universe that was created anew
With a majority then of but one
How can I live amongst those I created?
When they are but part of my thoughts.

A drama repeated through the ages
Played out once more then before me
Trapped are these the many players
Am I but one of they, that I guide?

Five final stars that beckon
These I add to my universe
One for each time in my misery
That I have laid a world to waste.

Confusion that reigns supreme
Chaotic in my mind and soul
The turmoil stirs my dread unfolding
With my fears of tomorrow not stilled.

I'm too tired it seems to stand up
To the drifting pace of change
Past habits now tend to guide me
Through all of my long yesterdays.

Binding me falsely into place
Are unseen thoughts deep within me?
Unable to counteract, held motionless
Imagined dangers now coming true.

Perils of feeling trapped
Longing to climb back to before
I see before me a new morning
Without fear of contradiction at last.

Longing to be free
And put an end to this adventure
I am challenged by the fates
To live out this tragedy.

Still my people move ever outward
To world and dreams left vacant for them
While new storms rage against inner defenses
The outward calm drives them always on.

My hopes for them remains intact
Though many trials have ended falsely
Craven deep with their minds patterns
Are images of my souls request?

For their destiny now must lie
Though always in a changing place
To find a path in stone to follow
Long since cast before them, it strays.

Side passages many they try to take
Each ends as always with the chosen
And with the variety of there changing moments,
What control I had once is long since vanished.

So with deepening doubts,

Of my own meager abilities.

Worlds collide often without meaning

Leaving lasting impressions not sought

# Chapter 6 ~ Growth of Civilization

Wisdom and knowledge shown by the stars
Possessed at first by the few
Now shared in full by the many
In richness and glory be.

The brevity of thought lengthens
Boosted in strength by my peoples growth
Each shares his thoughts with another
And in the greatness of learning brings more.

Civilization grows steadily outward
Expanding it's limits throughout space
The lengths of its horizons never shorten
A time that changes always forward.

One planet, then two, now three.
One system, then many are seen
Throughout the scope of mans endurance
In a galaxy that is their home to be.

Surpassing all limits before them
A universe beckons to all
And in conquering the millennia of time
In my pleasure I watch them grow.

The unchecked growth of my children
What these people have become in my stead
Would there be no limits placed upon them
Of their size and power to be gained.

Even now I feel within me
That they could reach out and touch my hand
I who had been their creator
Now stands scarcely above them all.

Now it seems that there has been lost
My place as their teacher ended
A spectator in a game I watch them all
With both admiration and envy regained.

So well had these children learned
Surpassing any limits that I set
Long past that which could have been reached
By those of my old world, enjoined.

This child created from my memory
Once as a thirstless student stood
Now surpassing even I as the teacher
Into an adulthood effortlessly moved.

With this growth in moments thought
Passing through eternities that I dreamed
The question of Justice now arises
And honor between all races of man.

Home system found in it's explorations
A lone planet called Basil by its own
With a people of man not so common
Unique in all things to come.

Their color was not as any other
A God's belief they had no question of
Yet living in peace did they always
Forsaking all alien ways and customs.

The first to discover found a society
That welcomed all visitors as brothers
But keep their ships at a distance
No contamination could then be spread.

Of trade they had no inclination
Book learning was a trivial thing
Only to be left alone was their dream
Far from any path of outside endeavor.

Yet the people of Basil held a treasure
An important mineral wanted by all
A key to future travel beyond the stars
How could these people refuse?

The honor of a system was held highest
By those of Home over any single thing
Yet the needs of the many outspoken
Could overwhelm the desires of the few.

Through barter and bribe did Home
Attempt to gain what was needed so dear
Still the purity of Basil remained
The mineral, though needed, was not taken.

Though most of this, my civilization
Lived through the trust of each other
A few remained scattered still
Who would try to gain the advantage sought.

These few together landed on Basil
Plied the natives through mystery and drugs
To gain what it was they wanted
And destroy a people who stood in the way.

A land and people joined as one
Not one could be removed from the other
And through their evil depravity
Did these invaders try for a selfish gain.

A gain for all of creation
Riches for those who stole
One less planet left to enlighten
So their careless thoughts would go.

Home took wind of this incident
And in a selfless action took on
To rid Basil of these invaders
And clear its memory of the deed.

The resistance of Basil though tried
Was futile before the drugs used
It's people had gone to the death
Or of dying in unwanted misery.

Then the valorous Forces of Home
Guardians of peoples independence
Landed in numbers upon solemn Basil
Without warning to any opposed.

With the swiftness of the silent sword
And the shrills of many encounters
The hero warriors of Home
Laid waste to the invaders of Basil.

Of those who had tried in the takeover
To gain fortune at the pain of others
They were carried aloft without mercy
With only what they held in their hands.

Deposited were they then
Abandoned on a barren young world
To live their remaining years without comfort
Lord of all the gold in this place.

And the planet that was Basil lived on
As its air so tarnished with drug
Was cleansed of all its pollutants
By the victorious guardians of Home.

Basil's system was then sealed
Against any unwanted intrusion
Until it could completely regain
That which had been so ruthlessly torn away.

For on a million worlds indescribable
And most of the yet undiscovered
Home felt the mineral would be discovered
Without challenging the freedoms of others.

And is this naught what I have sought?
That which lays in the paths of my wisdom
A story of strengths to be gained
By the rebirth of a lost mans soul.

In trying for those answers unknown
Searching fo the questions unasked
My mind left all disassociated thoughts
Which were at once dispelled from my longings.

In serenity my mind lay at peace
Think back to what once was my place
Of that which had long ago cast me out
To a future that had been unforetold.

I saw now upon the paths of the heavens
Built by the thoughts of this new man
A bridge now set across the universe
As a journey now set to begin.

The world below me is peopled
By a race of greatness in thought
Now was the time to free them
To reign in the stars beyond.

The difficulty was great within me
After the effects that I had so long sustained
Yet I must release my hold upon them
Those who had once stood so far below me.

I knew now that with their strength
My controls however well intentioned
Could no longer have a hold upon them
Without destroying all that had been built.

Laws had been given to them
Laid out in stone to be obeyed
In their greatness I saw a reflection
Of how like myself they had grown.

# Chapter 7 ~ Birth of the Swarm

Born in the depths of nameless fears
Torn from a sun that had gone nova
I found now strewn in this universe
A thing evil as the spawn of Hell.

A slithering worm rises grotesquely to the stars
From the soggy morass that was it's home
Arching it's sickly white body upwards
Into the violence of the twice found night sky.

Higher it reaches above the dark ground
In undulating waves of putrid motion
As if nature at it's far most worst
Could stand no meaning nor guidance.

When as if in realization
Of what it was that had been created
A bolt of lightening shot down from above
And struck down this abomination.

An Abysmal creature that had long stirred
Its life toasted away to a charcoal brown
Ending what was an overly long existence
For the vilest of all my creations.

Recognized naught at the beginning
As that which could be an end to all
An emissary it was to be enjoined
Sent from Home to learn about anew.

And so it was with brandished wonder
Excitement increasing beyond the norm
That Gilderslove gazed newly upon them
Wonders through evil never seen before.

He who was late of Oniba,
In the vast sector of Home
Now rising in the righteous thought
On the grounds of one planet forsaken.

Standing in the presence mystified
He was brought before the one
Seen was the majestic image of Foolat,
Evil personified on planet unforetold.

Unraveling as strands in the Wind
Before the astonished Gilderslove's propriety
Were things that should never be seen
By the mortals of a world such as Home.

Emperor Foolat now stood closely before him
Grand guardian of all that was to see
Things that could nor should not ever be alive
And those things of any world not sane.

As Gilderslove saw he thought back to before
Standing now in this temple of horror
That he represented no vanquished man
Kneeling before the eyes of the conqueror.

Thoughts of the invaders first words
Spoken of goodwill between races
But these had been the lies of the serpents
And the spirits of the of the fallen he heard cry.

Of his race there was no longer but a past
The present destroyed in a moment
Of their future no honor in living
Now there was none to stand by.

Hunger caused by one thousand pains
Tormented screams of billions
Rolled past and through as if not there
By the evil serpents boiling swarm.

I leave now but for a moment
From the nightmare that is Gildersloves
To contemplate what it was that had happened
In this imperfect boundlessness before me.

Realities in a universe beyond control
The pain and suffering then could not be
I stand now high above them, undignified
As the last good will casts me out.

From the world in the beginning that was called Home
Shared at first by all of my people
I was unable to cope with their realities
And now they escape with certain insanity.

From the beginning as they had set out
My people of Home knew only honor
A colonization cast many outward
On a million waiting worlds they arrived.

Hundreds of their years passed in greatness
The exploits of conquest many times heard
But always in due pathways charted by me
And of the good that was created forthright.

It was from a birthright of strength
That the people of Home did grow mighty
But always still it was tempered
By the pangs of unconscious righteousness.

When the swarm was first encountered
By an exploration fleet both bold and brave
The first it is said without contradiction
Died both quickly and without comprehension.

Following word that was coming through slowly
Of a creation of mine evil throughout
How could I have missed it then so completely
In all of my cleansing actions gone before.

Battle fleets were very soon issued
But the visitors call was good
And they entered then unimpeded
To the heart that was said to be of gold.

With chance taken nothing to accomplish
Peace was to them only a token
The stillness of the night rewarded
The bravery of fools unlimited.

Planetfalls came with hands outspread
The Swarm held it's thoughts to themselves
Yet even in the beginning they were there
Cold hearts carrying malice towards all.

The Swarm came in numbers overwhelming
Soon filled the cities unwarned
When violence at last exploded
Over a populace unprepared to fight.

Extinguished first were cities major
Throughout every point in the quadrant
Only Home was spared of this destruction
As only it had the Swarm not enveloped.

The Swarm with numbers unknown
Swept like locusts throughout the stars
Leaving only violent ruin behind them
In their course of ageless destruction.

So Gilderslove was sent at last
To meet with the imperious Emperor Foolat
Hope was resting still upon his shoulders
That a weakness could be found within them.

The Emperor stood in barbaric splendor
Awing those whose presence he commanded
Yet Gilderslove did so refuse to yield
Still a freeman such as he was want to be.

Gilderslove in his brave standing
Felt a mocking deep within him
That Foolat for all his majesty
Was but an evil snake to be destroyed.

The Emperor in his ungraciousness
Stood quailing before the proud emissary
"Who was he, this Gilderslove," thought Foolat
To stand as an equal before the Swarm.

Six of six hands reached out
Fists clenched in balls of fury
And Gilderslove, Homes emissary
Was struck sprawling to the hard ground.

"Fool!" shouted the Emperor Foolat
Malicious thoughts abounding
"Think you are fit to stand as one,
equal to the greatness of the Swarm?"

The valiant Gilderslove strove to rise
Held pinioned down by one on each side
Diplomacy which had held but little hope
Now lay dashed on the floor beside him.

Still Gilderslove held out promise
That a serpent may be destroyed
By cutting off its onerous head
And letting the rest to wither and die.

In his pocket Gilderslove held a bomb
To press close to the evil Foolat
Though both hands were held fast beside him
He tried to gain the victory sought

"Oh  mighty Emperor Foolat"
Gilderslove cried, yet his voice proudly held
In pain as each arm was twisted back
To be broken in a short time it seemed.

"You misunderstand my mission before you
I of Home have been sent to learn
Of that greatness that now stands before me
That which we have come now to call the Swarm."

And Foolat upon hearing these words
Of flattery to his inner calling
Commanded the release of Gilderslove
Who rose unsteadily to his feet.

As Gilderslove rose so he spoke
Reaching into his right breast pocket
"A present have we sent in honor for you,
to match the imperial Grandeur of the Swarm."

The time that remained was brief
Gilderslove felt no pain in the effort
As the nuclear devise was exploded
Palace and grounds were equally destroyed.

And the Emperor of the Swarm, Foolat
Had passed on to his first beginnings
But a serpents body may have many heads
And the Swarm lived on more hungrily.

# Chapter 8 ~ Realization of the Fall

We join in now together
Upon this other plane of reality
An existence so different in place
Yet not so very far from our own.

Seeing now in what it lays
Our minds what it is to be revealed
With a testament of knowledge gained
To other ways long since withheld.

The ending seems clear in place
As all of time rushes in
The end of a brief moment forecast
That which will end so catastrophically.

Broad minds appeal to many
Torn apart by the masses still
While the stars collide above
To bring total darkness to all.

My goals may have been honorable
Of my deeds there has been only good
Yet my thoughts have turned to ashes
On a million darkened worlds.

Clear of all else it seemed
On a primordial plane they lay
I was cast forth to this place
Where nothing else now grows.

It had begun in stillness
That quiet of absolute solitude
With nothing but my thoughts and soul
To temper it's existence in space.

A universe that had beckoned to me
And lay whole within itself
Empty save then but for the wishes
Of a man who had lost his way.

The works of common man
With the ideas held by the Gods
Words that held no meaning
When they are always said in vain.

I called to the wind below me
Which knew me by my name
To be brought upon a vacant shore
Precursor of a cloudy shroud.

Raising to a greatness then attained
Glory were they beyond all horizons
Now plunging into chaotic despair
In all to short a time it fell.

Mysteries that surround their quest
Peace that is suddenly overcome
The madness of a moment lost
Ruptured by the fears of tomorrow.

Forbidden dreams that arise
Borne of many uncertainties
They land in the darkness of yesterday
When the morning will never arrive.

My people in their greatest day
Drew challenge upon challenge before them
And with each one in turn overcome
They drew further upon their chosen path.

And with each passing generation
My complacency became more complete
Till the day came without my knowledge
That my vision was channeled not only to good.

Beyond the reaches of Home
A holocaust had been stirring
Released from my bonds of holding
By the fears beyond tomorrow's means.

They began as any others
A people like all of my own
But created from my darker side
In the insecurities of my life before.

As Home was guided by my soul
The other drew power from my mind
In recesses that were long forgotten
A dreadful ordeal that took place.

Wisdom and knowledge forgotten
Blinders put over my eyes
They grew in ways not wanted
From the fears that I thought left behind.

A universe apart they grew
In numbers and power inconceivable
Till their own Armageddon overtook them
But the survivors they lived on.

Mutations of the most perverted kind
He who changed least ruled them all
And with this dangerous transformation
All remnants of humanity were lost.

Outward then they soon expanded
Outrageous in form and thought
Little now did they resemble those people
My humanity nurtured of Home.

How could I have missed them
Their formation within the midst
Of my greatest trial experiments
And the final expectations of my dreams.

And now the Swarm in it's fury
It's evil long-living emperor destroyed
Lived on in terrible anger
Destroying all that came before them.

My civilization that awaited at Home
In the mold that I had cast
Knew of no way desirable
To counter such a Swarm, so extreme.

Conflicts few and short lived
The lost ideals of the many
Could compare then lightly still
With the ordeal that was happening now.

Noble warriors of the Home guard
Trying to comprehend the Swarm
Drew their arms with so many good intentions
They were slaughtered before they could fire.

I recognized deep within me
From where the Swarm had come
Was it too late now to save my people
When all was gone now but Home.

I tried to interject without fortune
To give Home what it was that was needed
To fight for survival on equal terms
With the evil serpent called the Swarm.

But past guidelines still held fast
On what it was that I could create
They hobbled my effort to give Home
The needed edge before it was too late.

A warriors spirit of outrage
Fierce demands for independence still
Sharp eyes for a gunners range
And a mind whose wit would not crack.

But the Swarm in it's quantum moves
Left little for which Home to depend
Till finally they stood at the gate
With only Home's system not conquered.

I knew that my experiment had failed
For in escaping from my old life
And in creating a new world beyond it
I had only made the old mistake again.

My civilization of Home with it's glory
And preeminent rise to greatness
Had been shattered by something unspoken
Hidden behind all of my fears.

So now I watch the final chapter
As Home defends itself to the end
The conclusion reached was foregone
My civilization so proud would die.

# Chapter 9 ~ The Swarm's Evil Fury

Planets explode as starships fall
Heavens high to the gates of Hell
The Swarm lays forth it's challenge
Can the powers of old respond.

"Home, I cast out his challenge to you
try and end my reign of terror
It is the power of now that carries us
Which serves to guide one way.

Uncounted souls lay scattered
Deaths that may not be forgiven
Unrequented hatred cast out in fury
From journeys that were never ended.

"Serpent you shall never be forgiven
Of the evil quest you partake in
The ending is now near at hand"
Was the cry as the battle was enjoined.

One onto twelve
And twelve onto seven
Given forth their all
Was the city of Alabon.

Desperate was their plight
To stave off the evil horde
A moment needed to be gained
Their freedom to be ever lost.

Individual customs lay torn about
From Alabon ever to arise again
They leave their places many fold
A fight to enjoy peace once more.

Grimacing naught with no moral thought
At each atrocity gained
The lord of evil lears greedily
With each new act repeated.

The skies exploded with their million suns
As defenses roar to protection
Invasion tried or no landfall made
One planet rules, in no quadrant peace.

The invaders know only of fiery sword
And through the heavens sweep
Past all resistance futile made
To Heavens door they travel far.

Upon a bridge of gold and silver
Given command of death and ordeal
He who stands at the Thrown of Power
Carries the Aura of demons seed.

Crews that live in a nightmare
Driven only by their desire
Quenched in bloodshed shared hungrily
On every distant world destroyed.

As arrows were their warships forged
A bridgehead to Hells dominion
Destroying all who stand before them
"Who dare to resist the Swarm?"

And what of the who quail in fright
Who for peace at any price do surrender?
With any sacrifice or honor gained
For their own worlds last defense.

Cut down are they in untold numbers
In ways beyond any terror known
Says the Swarm; "None can deserve life
But for those who choose to defend it."

In the temple of the warship bridge
There stands a tyrant above them
Borne for a desire for achievement
Overcome by the elements of greed.

The planet lies helpless beneath them
Where children had once used to play
And to in the past daylight of wisdom
The riches of peace once lay about.

"One thousand ships shall be built
From the riches that lay below us
Great warships built to conquer
Laid on the bones of those who oppose."

"Defenseless now standing before us
A planet of gold lies awaiting
To plunder it in a way unholy
In this way lay our destiny to grow.

"Withhold nothing that we have
In the slaughter now commencing
As the more quickly that we conquer
The wider our empire spreads.

"Glory to all that stand with us
Of empires servants we have many
Honor to those who emerge with victory
With a place by the Emperors knee."

A single fighting ship remains
Of the once great fleet of Alabon
It's pilot standing in helpless awe
Beside a panel broken and twisted.

He watches the force fields glow
Dimmer with each passing moment
What glory can in death there be
He stands in transfixed horror.

Planets destroyed beneath
The way to Home now clear
The enemy fleet undiminished
By spectacular defense overcome.

The Captain turns around slowly
Facing his disheartened crew
The worn face of hopeless resignation
To a fate that now awaits before them.

With every effort they had tried
For every victory a loss followed
The enemy never grew tired
While the Home fleet came steadily undone.

Rage and bombs smashed briefly
From the Home fleet to enemy lines
Yet for every Swarm ship destroyed
70 more arose to take their place.

A broken line holds no resistance
A feint turns to open route
When tired defenders give up hope
And the Swarm moves in for the kill.

The odds had been insurmountable
The quality of Home shining not
For the numbers of the Swarm were greater
Than the stars they had left in the sky.

So the crew of the last defender
Crippled by too many blows
Watched the last of civilization
Fall beneath the Swarms outreaching hands.

# 10 ~ The Home Debates

A red cart ornately carved
Rolls down a blackened street
Strewn with the rubbish ungathered
Of countless hands thrown into defeat.

In a chamber deep beneath the surface
On a planet doomed to meet violent death
The Elders of Wisdom and Knowledge met
To be the holders of what truth remained.

Undertaking a task
More solemn than any
Where a move the wrong way
Will lead only to death.

A debate which stands before them
To decide in which issue the truth lay
The question of the scourge of violent evil
Should it be brought to an end at all costs.

What price is freedom
That cost that we pay
When we live out our lives
And tomorrow we stay.

Freedom or slavery
Is one better than the other
When slavery means to live
And to hold freedom is to die.

Is the life of a slave owned by a master
Worse than a man doomed to die
Too soon they will have to decide
The meaning of that word liberty.

Is a mans soul eternal
Living in freedom beyond death
Or are we forever to be damned
If we fail in the choices we make.

The choices made before them
Effecting the present of them all
The meaning can seem so lost today
When ordained from the paths once taken.

The table continues
The journey endless
As one thing leads
Always to another.

Individual freedoms gained
For Home never again held
Taken leave for the many suns
Enjoy a peace now lost.

"The future holds no more for us."
Said the leader of those resolved
In a secret meeting held below
"No hope for tomorrow shall there be."

"Yet within us here it seems
We hold a power far greater
Than this universe nor any other has seen
And in it's wisdom we can now lay before us.".

"Do we use this force we possess
To bring an end to never ending menace
When in all that we use to destroy it
May cause an end to all of creation."

"That way which now seems so clear'
carries us always to the ground before it
Can we make this decision so graven
That which leads us to this canyon of time."

"Our paths however created
They seemed often to lead us straight
This path to whom each that we now seek
And where we so cherish our dreams are lost."

"Think for a moment where we've been taken
as we hold on, if only a moment longer
to those breaths we had wished most in life for
and whom now be forever not forgotten."

There stood in the system called Home
From where all life had once begun
Still to be quieted was the many
By the conquering Swarm above.

Scholars were they all
Those who governed this land
To carry each mans knowledge
Through all creation was their goal.

"Now we must be strong." Ende the leader
In solemn twilight has spoken
"On this the last meeting of freedom
of the twice sure honored lords of Home."

Their spiritual strength was within them
That which stood for the universes guidance
Against this vast fleet spreading
Against odds of infinity will Home prevail.

But to stop the invaders they must
To protect all of the people was the pledge
As the worlds as yet not conquered
And for the children as not yet borne.

# 11 ~ End of a Universe

One had come to conquer
Determined to win throughout all worlds
One came as the vanquished
Its destiny at last to stop the horde.

Fleets once soared in the space around them
A dying light emerging from within
A race doomed to perish from thought.
In the brilliant light of it's soul.

Starships explode
In the violence of the moment
A race that had once grown old
It raised it shield twice beaten aside.

Swords cross on a violent night
Storms crash on a rocky shore
Planets in upheaval coughing up their dead
Stars in torment obscure the darkness.

Cities lay barren
Dashed by an imperative
A people doomed to conquest
A civilization destined to fall.

Shadows crossing a widening plane
A glowing star in the sky
Obscured by the darkening clouds
A sun tries to begin the day.

The darkness of the clouds prevails
Keeping the night from turning to day
And changes the paths of the universe
Where good is no longer enough.

Draw the page across the word
Leaving the changes behind
The sun has been lost in the morning
As the moons join the clouds over the dead.

Once the night became the Day
The forest came onto the water
What have you now but the thirst for one
And my longing for the other.

As the water had said once onto the forest
In peace and tranquility before them
I will guide my quenching power
To your roots where it is needed much.

And the forest had stood by the waters
Taking its place beneath the far mountains
Knowing it's place was secure
It's peace would stand forever.

Then one lone tree had dipped it's boughs
Into the water by lands end
There it had tried to take nourishment
That's it browning leave shown was denied.

But nourishment naught was there
Into this now poison brew
And the sea raged in fury
Against the land that now trembled.

Now it goes on through an inner course
No longer that path carved for man
Leading not where no one can know
On a quest for the knowledge of life.

With but a last fleeting thought
Of the greatness that had come before
The Elders of the planet Home
Called open their minds deepest recess.

Unleashing a torrent before them
Sweeping the plague from all known space
Caught in the edges amidst it
All that had stood good in it's place.

All power once held was lost
Powerless they stood amongst them
A universe once created of nothing
Now raced ever faster to it's doom.

Out of the sky above them
The clouds parted in turmoil
Lightness grew bold around them
As the stars together burst.

Brightness of a galaxy
Grown by courage many times over
Swallowing all before it
And showing no end to it's appetite.

In it's path layout many worlds
Of creation that had been made
Once grown to be great in thought
Destroyed by a weakness within.

Born into a great loss
This spawn of evil destroyed
To perish now forever graven
In the grandeur of a universes death.

The moon and seven stars bright
Red flames of a heavens on fire
Burning torrents of rage
That had filled the hearts of men.

Death lays all around them
As the carnage of the fiend
So much suffering came to so many
Dreams that have gone so wrong.

Much was hoped for in the beginning
But the fears of my mind torment
With all of it charges unforgiven
Had over whelmed all Gods creatured created.

An eternity now passes around them
On this world Home I had once created
Longing for a world made of heaven
Dashed against the rocks of sub-consciousness.

"It seems but yesterday I had begun
Creating a world of my dreams
In a universe which had lain empty
Except for the being that was I."

"Now around me crumbles this universe
Overcome by chaos and doubts
From that which I was unable to control
In the imperfect mind such as mine."

"Now my soul rebels
To that which I see around me
As I try to hold on without avail
Slipping away from my grasp is my universe."

As currents passing
Creating the image
Swirling water grown
Between what lay around them.

As stars began to die
A coalescence amongst them
Merging into few
Where there had once been many.

And in the edges still left untouched
These once had been Eller's sanctuary
They were torn in finality asunder
By opposing streams of forced thought

All that had been Eller
Was now carried away, gone
And a universe lay barren
But for emptiness once again.

# Chapter 12 ~ Eller's Nightmare

There is a beginning
And always an end
How is it then
That much comes between.

In the beginning was Eller
Lost in life was he
Swept into another place
Of his own making still.

While it is true that which was once done
But then lost in what is real
To someone who no longer cares
Of his place within our world.

That he who had intended no grief
Yet the pain is there to feel
Can a people not grow forever and give
Without the unhappiness of this despair?

What sayeth thee now people
On a thousand dying worlds
Crying out Eller's name in vain
Do they not know to whom they call.

The horror of Eller's reality
What had been created but not set within
The specter of mans inhumanity
"why did I create that which I did?"

A dreamquest, So it had once begun
Creating the beautiful from the old
Wonder in the eyes within him.
Engagement in this universe alone.

Through the pitfalls and the quandaries
To beginning something new
To find where it is to start
A beginning has no emotions running deep.

Tears came to the eyes of Eller
As he watched his people die
Torn of the violence within him
Victims of the chaos of his own mind.

"For I am no man", Eller shouts
"And I have discovered I am no God'
Who is to guide me in the path
In that of which I choose to seek."

First and last always
Ones with an eternity
What is it that all men can bring
To this universe that is gone.

An idealism lost, torn asunder
By the events Eller could not control
That life he had created to freedom given
And lost from Eller's torn soul.

Between the universe of our own bodies
And another as real of our souls
There exists yet another fully
Of reality not, but truly real.

False in it's perceptions
To those who seek refuge in it
And fatal to those who fail
To appreciate its seriousness.

On the thin line of boundary
Between the real and unreal
Imagination and tranquility
Eller stepped into the void.

Creating in his mind a world
A universe wholly real to him
As the universe you and I live in
Real in all its tragedies borne to us.

A world not solely of Eller's mind
Nor only of his body too
Somewhere in between a temporal state
Impossible for mortal man to conceive.

Such division had brought more distance
From the hopes that Eller once held
What gains there were in the beginning
Were lost in the imperfection of the soul.

# Chapter 13 ~ Epilog

And as a God could weep
So did Eller cry
As he fell through a darkness
That carried him back.

Homeward bound at last
His thoughts touched on distant memories
How was it before he left
What seemed an eternity before.

Universe of his creating
To return now from where he had gone
No longer with any other choice
His own creations had failed him.

Casting back now through a door
To a present that had been forgotten
How much time had passed in crossing
Will he recognize from where he had come?

You may ask why I have written this
For you? And I answer it is for me.
We all have our past lives mysteries
And guarded dreams unresolved.

But for Eller our hero what more can be said
That can be put down for our eyes to see
Taken for granted, left without regard
An Idea never planted will never be.

And could it not be
That we ourselves it may seem
And the world imagined
And the universe perceived.

Are but the dreams, delusions molded

Of a man deemed once insane

As Eller so it seemed

In another's place and time believed?

## Coming This Spring 2006 Confessions of a Virgin Sacrifice

**By Adrianne Ambrose**

Sound the alarm! Saddle the horses! Wake up the Village Elders! The Sacrificial Virgin has escaped!

Jezebelle's cousin Diz is slated for a sacrificial swan dive into the local volcano. Not if Jez can help it! But, things go horribly wrong, and now the gals are on the run, with the furious Village Elders in hot pursuit!

Jez sweeps her cousin on a whirlwind adventure through the jungle and beyond, with nothing but her sardonic wit and bronze brassiere at her disposal. Along the way the two attract a motley cast of characters including a brooding barbarian with decidedly unheroic phobias, an ill-tempered troll looking for love, and a deadly Blue Wolf with a soft spot for Jezebelle.

Throughout their travel, Jez untangles the clues to her True Destiny. She discovers a Forbidden Secret that threatens to unravel the very fabric of her world - or at least ruin her day.

## Coming This Spring 2006
## Apers

**By Mark Jansen**

Time: near future

Place: California' Central Valley

FarmTek Industries, conducts controversial genetic engineering research.

Their Mission: create a new order of life as a source of manual labor for the agricultural industry.

Mirabella : the first successful Aper. An unintended consequence... her high level of intelligence.

Her world changes when she discovers pruning.

Then young Aper ventures alone into the outside world. There she meets 3 young teenagers who help her bring the truth of Apers to the world.